CLICK, CLACK, MOO
Cows That Type

For my Dad – D.C.
To Sue Dooley – B.L.

SIMON AND SCHUSTER UK LTD
1st Floor, 222 Gray's Inn Road, London WC1X 8HB

First published in Great Britain in 2002 by Simon & Schuster UK Ltd
Paperback edition published in 2002 by Pocket Books

A CIP catalogue record for this book is available from the British Library

ISBN 978-1-471-14688-6

Printed in Malaysia

1

CLICK, CLACK, MOO
Cows That Type

by Doreen Cronin   pictures by Betsy Lewin

SIMON AND SCHUSTER

Farmer Brown has a problem.
His cows like to type.
All day long he hears

Click, clack, **moo.**
Click, clack, **moo.**
Clickety, clack, **moo.**

At first, he couldn't believe his ears.
Cows that type?
Impossible!

Click, clack, **moo.**
Click, clack, **moo.**
Clickety, clack, **moo.**

Then, he couldn't believe his eyes.

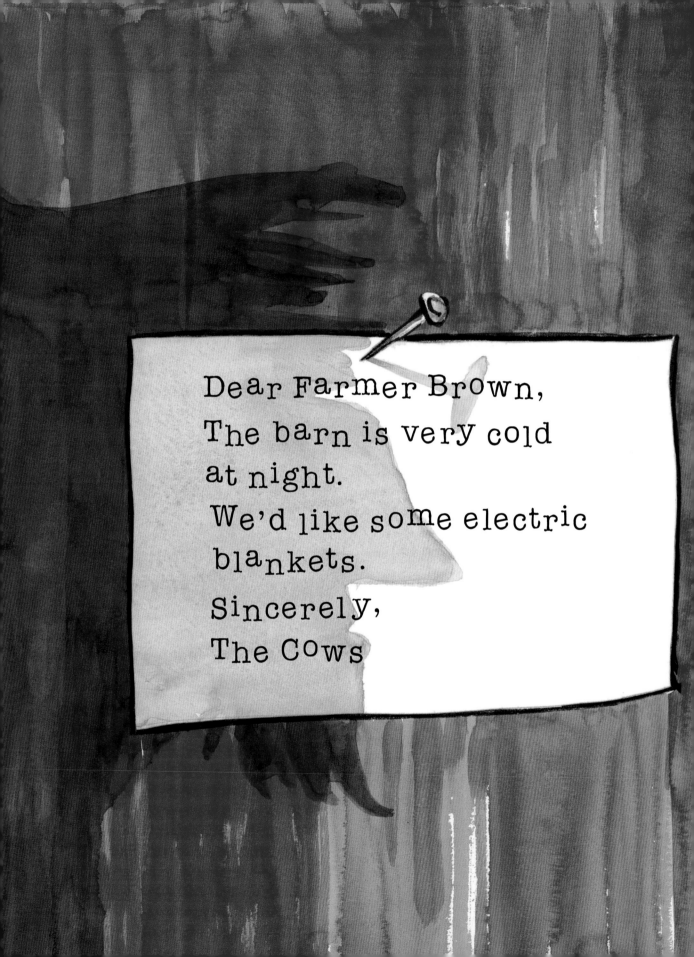

It was bad enough the cows had found the old typewriter in the barn, but now they wanted electric blankets! "No way," said Farmer Brown. "No electric blankets."

So the cows went on strike. They left a note on the barn door.

"No milk today!" cried Farmer Brown. In the background, he heard the cows busy at work:

Click, clack, **moo.**
Click, clack, **moo.**
Clickety, clack, **moo.**

The next day, he got another note:

Dear Farmer Brown,
The hens are cold too.
They'd like electric blankets.
Sincerely,
The Cows

The cows were growing impatient with the farmer. They left a new note on the barn door.

"No eggs!" cried Farmer Brown.
In the background he heard
them.

Click, clack, **moo.**
Click, clack, **moo.**
Clickety, clack, **moo.**

"Cows that type. Hens on strike! Whoever heard of such a thing? How can I run a farm with no milk and no eggs!" Farmer Brown was furious.

Farmer Brown got out his own typewriter.

Dear Cows and Hens:

There will be no electric blankets.
You are cows and hens.
I demand milk and eggs.

Sincerely,
Farmer Brown

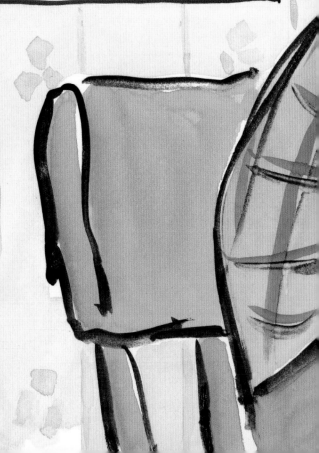

Duck was a neutral party, so he brought the ultimatum to the cows.

The cows held an emergency meeting. All the animals gathered around the barn to snoop, but none of them could understand Moo.

All night long, Farmer Brown waited for an answer.

Duck knocked on the door early the next morning. He handed Farmer Brown a note:

Farmer Brown decided this was
a good deal. He left the blankets

next to the barn door and waited for
Duck to come with the typewriter.

The next morning he got a note:

Dear Farmer Brown,
The pond is quite boring.
We'd like a diving board.
Sincerely,
The Ducks

Click, clack, **quack.**
 Click, clack, **quack.**
Clickety, clack, **quack.**